WINDSURFING WINNER

BY JAKE MADDOX

ILLUSTRATED BY SEAN TIFFANY

text by Thomas Kingsley Troupe

Jake Maddox books are published by Stone Arch Books
A Capstone Imprint
151 Good Counsel Drive, P.O. Box 669
Mankato, Minnesota 56002
www.capstonepub.com

*Library of Congress Cataloging-in-Publication Data is available on the
Library of Congress website.*

Library Binding: 978-1-4342-2535-1

Summary: Nick gives up everything he tries. So when he's on vacation, he
tries surfing. He doesn't like it, so he quits. A friendly girl helps him learn
to windsurf. But will he quit that if he can't do it?

Art Director: Kay Fraser
Graphic Designer: Hilary Wacholz
Production Specialist: Michelle Biedscheid

Photo Credits: Sean Tiffany (cover, p. 1)

Printed in the United States of America in Stevens Point, Wisconsin.
092010
005934WZS11

TABLE OF CONTENTS

CHAPTER 1

NOT READY

Nick had never been anywhere so beautiful in his whole life. For years, he and his family had wanted to visit Hawaii. Now they were finally there, spending a whole week in Honolulu. The weather was awesome, and Nick was glad to be on vacation, but he wasn't having a great time.

The island was perfect, but Nick's older brother, Eric, didn't seem impressed.

"The longer we stand here, the less time we'll have in the water," Eric said, picking up his surfboard. "Come on, let's find the rest of the class."

Nick nodded. They were supposed to get a lesson on surfing before tackling the waves. It was free with their surfboard rentals.

"There they are," Nick said, pointing. A dozen new surfers were lined up on the beach.

Eric ran down the wooden steps to the sand, carrying his board. But Nick walked down slowly, afraid he'd slip and fall in front of a bunch of strangers.

He didn't know if he'd like surfing, but it was worth a shot. After all, they were on vacation.

Nick's dad had wanted to go scuba diving, which sounded like fun to Nick, but the hotel didn't offer lessons to anyone under fifteen.

Nick's mom was happy to listen to music and read by the pool. She wasn't a fan of sand. The other option was synchronized swimming. No thanks.

So Nick picked surfing, mostly because Eric had. He only hoped he'd be good at it. Otherwise, it would be a long week with no other activities to try.

"Let's go, slowpoke!" Eric called from the beach. He and all of the other surfers watched as Nick carefully walked down the stairs. He knew he was holding up the lesson, so Nick tried to run with his surfboard like Eric had. But he slipped.

He fell down onto the hot sand, face first. His board fell down on top of him.

The instructor ran over and helped Nick up. Once Nick was on his feet, the instructor picked up his board.

"I'm Kenji," the instructor said. Kenji was tan and wore a shark-tooth necklace around his neck. "I'll teach you how to surf. Maybe you'll even learn some balance."

Nick said, "I hope so." He smiled. Kenji seemed nice, even if he was sort of making fun of him.

Nick brushed the sand off of his swim trunks and face. Then he followed Kenji back to the rest of the group.

I'm not off to a very good start, Nick thought. *I'm not even in the water yet, and already I don't like this.*

The other surfers were still waiting. All of them seemed at least five years older than Nick.

"Smooth moves, baby brother," Eric whispered. "Real smooth."

Nick ignored his brother. He set his board down on the sand next to him.

The lesson went very quickly. They learned about the different parts of the board, including the leash. Nick didn't think he'd like having a strap tying him to the surfboard, but he also didn't want to lose the rented board. He knew his dad would be mad if he did.

Kenji showed them how to paddle out, how to stand up on the board, and the difference between a "regular foot" stance and "goofy foot."

Goofy foot meant that the right foot was forward. Every surfer stood one way or the other.

"Why am I not surprised you're a goofy foot?" Eric said, pointing at Nick's feet.

"Quit teasing me," Nick said. He tried standing the other way, but it didn't feel right.

"I think we're ready," Kenji said. "Let's catch some waves."

Everyone seemed ready to hit the ocean. Everyone, that is, except Nick.

CHAPTER 2

QUITTING TIME

Surfing was a disaster. Eric picked it up right away. He was great at it. But Nick wasn't so lucky.

He paddled out with the rest of the group, but had trouble turning his board around. When a good wave came, it was hard for him to get up on his feet. Every time he finally made it and was standing on his surfboard, he lost his balance and fell off.

More than a few times, the board smacked Nick on the head. He knew he'd have bruises.

"How's it going?" Eric asked as he paddled toward him at the end of the lesson. Nick was busy wiping his hair from his eyes and spitting out water.

"Fantastic," Nick said, rolling his eyes. "I've never had so much fun."

It was the worst time he'd ever had. It was worse than the entire baseball season when he couldn't get a hit. And it was worse than when he tried out for football but dropped the ball every time he had it.

"You're going to quit, aren't you?" Eric said, shaking his head. "You always quit."

Nick scowled. *It's not my fault I'm not as good at stuff as Eric is*, he thought.

"I'm going to keep trying," Nick insisted.

"You better," Eric said. "Dad will be mad if you just quit. He paid for you to surf all week."

A week of this? Nick thought. *This will be the worst vacation ever.*

* * *

No one could say Nick didn't try. Not even Eric.

He paddled back toward the waves and tried his best, but nothing went right. A giant wave knocked him down. The board hit him on the head again. His eyes felt raw and stung from the salt water.

Everyone else was having a great time. Eric rode giant waves back to the beach. He never fell more than a few times. Nick's older brother was a natural.

Nick only got more upset.

Finally, he'd had enough. "I'm going back to the beach," Nick said. He passed Eric, who was paddling back out to catch another wave. "I'll see you later."

"You're quitting, aren't you?" Eric asked. He shook his head.

"Mind your own business," Nick snapped. "Surfing stinks."

* * *

A little bell on the door of Don's Surf Shop jingled as Nick pushed it open. It was hot outside, but the air conditioning inside made him shiver. He didn't care. He just wanted to turn in the surfboard and get it over with.

The guy who had rented the boards to Nick and Eric the day before wasn't there.

Instead, a girl wearing a red wetsuit stood behind the counter.

"Hi," said the girl. "Can I help you?"

"Yeah," Nick said. "I need to return this surfboard."

The girl nodded. She typed something into the computer. It beeped, and she looked at the screen, puzzled. "You're returning the board early?" she asked.

You didn't see me out there, Nick thought. *I looked like a complete fool!*

"Yeah," Nick replied. "I guess I just don't like surfing."

"Got it," the girl said. "Unfortunately, we have a policy that there aren't any refunds. I'm sorry."

"That's fine," Nick said. He shrugged.

He knew Dad would be mad, but he didn't feel like being even more embarrassed. "It doesn't matter," he added. "I just want to return the dumb thing."

"Tell you what," the girl said. "I've got a better idea. Come with me."

Nick set the board against the counter and followed the girl into the back room of the surf shop.

CHAPTER 3

MEET MEIKO

Nick stepped into a large room loaded with surfboards, body boards, and some other ocean gear for rent.

"Wow," Nick whispered. "This place has a lot of stuff."

"I know," the girl said. "My dad overdid it when he opened this place."

Nick shook his head. "I guess you probably like surfing then, right?"

The girl shrugged. "It's okay," she said. "But I like windsurfing better. I bet you will, too."

"Is that where you have a parachute on your back and a boat flies you up in the sky?" Nick asked. He shook his head. "Forget that. I'm afraid of heights."

"No, that's parasailing," the girl said with a laugh. "Windsurfing is completely different."

Nick crossed his arms. He was pretty sure he wouldn't like anything that had to do with any kind of surfing.

"Just give it a shot," the girl said, smiling. "I'm Meiko, by the way."

She stuck out her hand, and Nick shook it. "I'm Nick," he told her. "Nice to meet you."

"Over here," Meiko said. She led him over to the back part of the room, past long boards and short boards. There, she pointed at different-looking surfboards and small sails.

"These are windsurfing boards," she said. "It's almost like riding a mini sailboat."

"It looks pretty cool," Nick said. "I'm just not sure I'd be any good at it."

"I'll teach you," she said.

Meiko pulled a blue windsurfing board off the wall. Then she lifted a sail from a metal rack.

Nick sighed. He didn't want to do any more surfing of any kind. With or without a sail. As far as he was concerned, he'd never be a surfer.

"I have to meet my family for lunch," Nick said. It sounded like a lie, but it was the truth. Mom and Dad wanted them to check in from time to time, and they had lunch plans.

"Perfect," Meiko said. "I get off at one. Stop by when you're done eating."

* * *

Nick walked back to the hotel. The whole time, he tried to figure out how he was going to get out of going back to the surf shop. It was nice of Meiko to offer lessons, but he wasn't interested. *I'm not meant to surf,* he thought.

Mom and Dad were waiting with Eric on the patio when Nick reached the restaurant. Shaded with a grass roof, the dining area overlooked the ocean.

Nick took a seat so that his back faced the blue waters. He didn't want to see the waves anymore.

"How did the morning go, boys?" Dad asked. He was still wearing his wetsuit and had goggle marks around his eyes.

"Awesome," Eric said right away. His hair was wet and his nose was red. "Wasn't it, Nick?"

Nick shrugged and looked down at the menu. "It was okay," he said.

Mom looked around. "You didn't leave your surfboard at the beach, did you, honey? Someone might walk off with it," she said. "That cost us a lot of money to rent."

"Yeah, Nick," Eric said. He laughed. "Where is your board?"

Nick sipped his water. "It's at the surf shop," he said. "I'm trading it for a different one."

"How come?" Dad asked. He looked at the beach. Nick could tell his dad was excited to get back into the ocean.

"His surfboard was broken," Eric joked. "It kept making him fall off!"

Mom swatted Eric with her napkin and said, "Be nice."

"I just needed something different," Nick said. "My first surfboard wasn't a good fit."

Everyone else ordered lunch, talking excitedly about what they'd done that morning. As he watched his parents and brother laugh and talk, Nick wondered how he'd keep busy for the rest of the week. His island vacation was off to a bad start.

CHAPTER 4

A BAD STUDENT

After lunch, Mom, Dad, and Eric took off. Nick wandered around the town. He didn't mean to, but at about 1:15, he found himself standing in front of Don's Surf Shop.

"Hey, Nick!" a girl's voice called. He turned and saw Meiko walking out of the shop. She smiled and waved, and added, "How was lunch?"

"It was okay," Nick said.

Meiko looked around. "Want to get started?" she asked.

Nick felt his stomach sink. He didn't want to get started. But was there a way to tell her that without hurting her feelings?

"About the windsurfing," Nick began. "I'm not sure . . ."

But then he noticed the pile of equipment next to her. Two boards. Two sails. And a bunch of other stuff.

"My dad said we could switch the surfboard rental for the windsurfing rig," Meiko said. "So I brought it all for you." She pointed to the gear on the ground.

Nick looked at the different parts and pieces. There were ropes, a board, foot straps, and a life vest. It seemed way more complicated than regular surfing.

It's not like I have anything better to do, Nick thought. "What is all this stuff?" he asked.

"You should learn the different parts and pieces of the rig," Meiko said. She started lifting up the different pieces of equipment and telling him about each one. Nick listened as she explained everything. "Okay, now we can put it all together!" Meiko told him. "Pick up the mast."

"That's this long pipe thing, right?" Nick asked.

Meiko grinned. "You were paying attention!" she teased. "Yes, that one."

Nick slipped the long pipe, called the mast, into the sail's sleeve. After that, he attached it to the middle of the board.

"Perfect," Meiko said. "So far so good."

Nick nodded. *Sure,* he thought. *Until I have to get this thing in the water.*

"Okay," Meiko continued. "See those black foot straps on the board? You slip your feet in there, and they help you stay on."

There were three foot straps, two in the middle and one at the nose of the board. They had a foam-like rubber covering.

"Hop on," Meiko said. "Let's see if we need to adjust anything."

Nick put his feet through the straps. They were actually pretty comfortable. "Nice," he said. "I couldn't stay on the regular surfboard. I kept slipping off."

Meiko laughed. "I had the same problem," she said. "I also like holding on to something."

"What do you hold on to when you're windsurfing?" Nick asked.

Meiko bent over. She pointed to a curved piece attached to the sail. It had a clip on one end.

"This is the boom," she said. "You use this to steer the sail. You raise the sail rig with a line called the uphaul," she went on. "The mast bends at the base, so if the sail falls, the board doesn't tip over."

"Cool!" Nick said. "That sounds perfect for me."

"Try raising the sail up," Meiko suggested. "Grab the uphaul, and pull it toward you."

Little by little, Nick pulled the sail off of the sand. When the sail was upright, he grabbed the boom.

"Excellent," Meiko said. She clapped. "You're on your way!"

Just then, a strong gust of wind picked up from behind them. It hit the sail and jerked Nick right off of the board. The sail went down, knocking Nick to the sand.

"Maybe that's enough for today," Meiko said as she helped him up. "Come back tomorrow morning, and we'll do more."

I can't even stay up on the beach, Nick thought. He spit out sand and brushed himself off. *How can I do this on the water?*

CHAPTER 5

NOT AGAIN

The next morning, Nick made a decision. He wouldn't embarrass himself and try windsurfing anymore. It was too hard, and he didn't want to waste Meiko's time.

"Should we meet again for lunch?" Dad asked at breakfast. He was drinking a glass of orange juice and looking at a map on the table. "I should be done with my next dive by then."

"Sounds good," Nick said as he pulled on a shirt.

Eric came out of the bathroom, brushing his teeth. "Did you switch surfboards?" he asked. "I haven't seen your new one yet."

"I'm picking it up this morning," Nick said. That was sort of true. He gave Eric a dirty look. "They found a shorter one for me to use."

"That's weird," Eric said, pretending to be confused. "I thought only experienced surfers used shorter boards."

"Quiet, Eric," Nick whispered.

Dad mumbled something as Mom fiddled with the television remote, trying to find the weather channel. "Just be careful out there," she said. "Don't get eaten by a shark!"

Everyone laughed. Nick laughed too, but he was already wishing the day was over.

* * *

"Just admit it. You quit," Eric said as he and Nick headed to the beach. Eric's surfboard was waxed and ready to go.

Nick groaned. "I didn't quit, okay?" he said. "I'm trying something else."

"Like what? Chess? You'd probably quit that, too," Eric said. "You quit everything you start."

"Whatever," Nick replied. He turned around and headed back toward the hotel, leaving his brother on the sidewalk.

I don't need to listen to him, he thought. But as he reached the entrance to the hotel, he felt guilty.

Meiko was waiting for him. She was probably waiting alone near the surf shop, the windsurf rig set up, wondering if Nick would come back.

He looked out at the beach. Everyone else was swimming, surfing, and having fun. *You didn't even try this time*, Nick reminded himself. *You fell once and decided to quit.*

Nick had quit lots of other things in the past. He'd joined the tennis team and quit. He'd tried out for a play and quit. He'd quit the science club after one day. He didn't want his vacation to be another example. *Not this time,* he thought.

He touched the bruises on his head from the surfboard. Then he turned and headed back out to the beach.

CHAPTER 6

RIDE THE WIND

"I was about to give up on you," Meiko said as Nick walked up to the surf shop. "I even brought you a wet suit!" she added.

She handed Nick a black suit. It had a zipper up the back and red stripes that went up the side.

"This is really cool," Nick said. "Thanks. And I'm sorry I'm late. I wasn't sure I'd be back. I guess I was pretty frustrated yesterday."

Meiko nodded. "I understand," she said. "But that was the first time you ever stood on the board! You'll get better with practice, and the first time you succeed, you'll forget about all of this."

She smiled. Then she added, "Besides, you haven't gotten to see how much fun windsurfing is yet!"

"Yeah, you're right," Nick said. "I never thought of it like that. The part about getting better, I mean."

"Go put on your wetsuit," Meiko said. "There are changing rooms around back. I'll meet you down by the beach."

* * *

The wetsuit made Nick feel like a superhero. But he didn't think it would help him become a better windsurfer.

After they found a place on the beach that wasn't full of swimmers or surfers, Meiko showed Nick how to drag the board and rig out to the water. They had to keep the sail down so the wind wouldn't catch it on the beach.

"Okay," Meiko said. "Now we have to check to see which direction the wind is going."

Nick looked back at the palm trees closer to the hotels. They swayed back and forth in the wind. He couldn't tell which direction the wind was coming from. It seemed like it was coming from all over.

"Here's what I do," Meiko said. She wet her fingertip on her tongue and then held it in the air. "You can feel which way the air's coming from. Southwest winds. That'll be perfect."

Together, they slid the board and sail into the water. Meiko held it steady while Nick hopped up onto the board. He was about to slip his feet into the foot straps when Meiko stopped him. "Not yet," she said. "You need to pull up the sail first."

Nick followed her directions, carefully keeping his balance. He bent forward and grabbed the uphaul line. Little by little, he pulled the sail upright.

"As you bring it up, steer the board so the nose faces the water," Meiko said. "It's kind of tricky."

Nick took small steps, and the board turned nice and slow. Once the sail was up, he held onto the boom.

"Like this?" Nick asked, looking down at Meiko, who stood in waist-deep water.

"Perfect," she said.

Without warning, the wind picked up. It filled the sail. Nick quickly slipped his feet into the straps. Grasping the boom, he turned it toward the ocean.

"Hey!" Nick cried. "I'm surfing! I mean, windsurfing!"

Meiko cheered for him. Nick looked back in excitement, totally unprepared for the big wave rushing toward him. It struck the nose of the board hard, knocking Nick into the ocean.

CHAPTER 7

BACK ON BOARD

Nick was underwater for a moment. Water rushed into his nose. Then he felt a hand grab the back of his wetsuit and pull him up. Just as he popped out of the water, another wave hit him, filling his mouth with water. He almost went back under.

"Are you okay?" Meiko asked, treading water near him.

"Yeah," Nick said, then coughed his throat clear. "I'm fine."

"I'm sorry," Meiko said. "I didn't see the wave coming. If you want to stop or whatever —"

"Are you kidding?" Nick shouted. "That was awesome! I want to go again!"

The board and sail hadn't drifted too far away. Nick swam over and climbed on. With Meiko's help, he was ready for a second attempt.

"To make sharp turns, just hold the boom, keep your feet in the straps, and lean back," Meiko said. "It'll help you avoid waves."

Nick nodded. He tried to lean back. It felt like he would tip over, but he didn't. The board angled slightly, cutting into the water.

No more big waves for me, he thought.

The wind was calmer now. Nick skimmed across the water pretty easily. He watched the surfers farther down the beach. Every few seconds, one of them wiped out.

Nick angled himself out a bit farther and learned to turn the board as the bigger waves came. Instead of hitting them head on, he rode them back toward Meiko, who smiled proudly.

"You're doing great," Meiko said. "I've never taught anyone before!"

"Really?" Nick asked. "I kind of thought it was part of your job, like renting surfboards and selling swimsuits."

"You're my first student," Meiko admitted. "I didn't want to tell you before."

"I'm impressed," Nick told her. "Anyone who can get me to windsurf has to be good."

"Yeah, next thing we know, you'll be doing forward flips," Meiko said, laughing.

Nick frowned. "What's a forward flip?" he asked.

"Don't worry," Meiko said. "I don't think I can teach you that. That's a way more advanced trick. Let's just focus on surfing for now."

Nick practiced shifting the rig to catch the wind. Just when he thought the wind died, it picked up again. After only a few wipeouts, he was ripping back and forth along the waves.

They took a break, and Nick dragged the board and rig up onto the beach. Then he collapsed in the sand.

"I think I'm going to miss windsurfing when I get home," Nick admitted.

"You don't have to," Meiko said. "If you've got lakes nearby, you can still windsurf. Of course, the waves aren't the same."

Nick laughed. "I'm not a fan of the big waves anyway," he said.

Meiko glanced at her waterproof watch. "Oh, it's almost one," she said. "I need to get back. My dad is waiting for me to take the counter for a while."

One o'clock? Nick couldn't believe it. He was late for lunch!

CHAPTER 8

ISLAND TOUR

Eric was just finishing his burger when Nick arrived. Mom and Dad both looked a little upset.

"Where have you been?" Eric asked.

"We agreed we'd all check in at noon and eat together," Dad said. "It's almost one thirty!"

"Sorry, Dad," Nick said. He couldn't help but smile.

Getting in trouble was worth it. He'd finally found something he really liked to do. The best part? He wasn't too bad at it!

"So?" Eric asked again. "Where were you?"

"Oh, you know," Nick said, still smiling. "Surfing."

"Yeah, right," Eric muttered. Even though Eric kept asking questions, Nick wouldn't tell him anything. It was fun to keep his older brother guessing.

* * *

After lunch, Nick's family decided to tour the island together to see some of the sights. Dad wanted to drive up into the hills to take pictures. Mom wanted to go to the marketplaces to find souvenirs to take home.

Eric thought it would be cool to see the volcano. While Nick thought the sights were interesting, he just wanted to get back to the beach. He couldn't wait to catch the wind and ride along the waves.

After sightseeing, they all went out to a fancy dinner. Nick couldn't stop looking at his watch. It was getting darker outside, and he wondered if he'd be able to get back and windsurf again before it was too dark.

Once they were finally back at the hotel, the sun had almost sunk below the horizon. Mom, Dad, and Eric stayed in the room to watch a movie, but Nick had other plans. He zipped up his wetsuit and ran down to the beach, heading for the surf shop.

Once there, he saw Meiko's dad locking up the front door.

"Hi," Nick called. "Are you guys closed?"

Meiko's dad nodded. He said, "Until tomorrow morning. Sorry."

Nick's heart sank. There were only a few more days left of vacation. As he turned to head back, Nick heard a familiar voice call, "Hey, Nick!"

Nick turned. It was Meiko. She had her wetsuit on and was dragging a board and rig toward the water.

"Grab yours," she said. "Hurry! While there's still light."

While the sun set, Nick and Meiko windsurfed together across the bright orange and red waves. The sunset colors made it seem like they were sailing across a different world.

CHAPTER 9

Before Nick knew it, it was his final day on the island. He was grateful to have spent a lot of time in the ocean, but sad he'd be leaving the next morning.

"You're lucky," Nick said to Meiko as they pulled their boards into the water that morning. "You get to live here."

Meiko laughed. "Everyone thinks life is a vacation here," she said. "But I still go to school and work, just like anywhere else."

Nick squinted at Meiko. "Really? It's not extra cool to live here?" he asked.

"Okay," Meiko admitted. "It pretty much is the best place to live."

The sky was cloudy, and the wind felt stronger. Nick was careful not to turn his sail so that the wind would be directly behind him. Even so, he tore along the water much faster.

Nick watched the surfers down the beach. He was glad he'd learned to windsurf. And mostly he was glad he hadn't quit just because at first it had been hard.

* * *

After lunch that day, Nick went up to the hotel room and got his digital camera. He wanted a photo of himself windsurfing.

When Nick got back to the beach, Meiko was waiting for him. "Good news," she said. "My dad gave me the rest of the day off. We can windsurf until you're sick of it!"

"Not possible," Nick said, smiling. "You know, I never did thank you for showing me how to do all this. I was ready to quit after that first day. Now, I can't get enough!"

Meiko smiled. "No problem," she said.

"Would you mind taking a few pictures of me out there?" Nick asked. "I want to prove to my friends that I actually windsurfed out here. They probably wouldn't believe me otherwise."

Meiko nodded and took the camera. As Nick pushed the board and rig out, a familiar person surfed toward him.

Eric, Nick thought. *Great. That's all I need. I'm not going to let him wreck my last run.*

Nick climbed onto his board and pulled up the rig.

"Hey, Nick!" Eric called, shredding past. "Don't fall!"

Nick ignored him and grabbed the boom. Just then, an insane wind blew out from the beach. Before he could do anything, Nick was cruising toward some choppy waves. *Uh-oh*, Nick thought. *This doesn't look good.*

Nick held onto the boom as tight as he could. He tried to turn the sail but couldn't. The wind rocketed him closer to the coming crests.

Great, Nick thought. *Meiko will snap a picture of me crashing and looking dumb!*

CHAPTER 10

PHOTO OP

At that moment, the nose of the board struck the wave hard. Nick braced for impact. He felt the hit in his arms, and his legs wavered. The entire board and rig flew into the air. The world spun upside down as he waited for the crash.

Nick knew what would happen. His mouth and nose would fill with water. The sea would smack against his skin.

And Eric and Meiko would laugh at him.

Nick closed his eyes, bracing for the impact. He tried to move his body so that the board would stay even.

When he opened them, the world was right-side up. The board slapped down on the water, and he was still sailing out.

"Whoa," Nick gasped.

He leaned back and turned the board around, cutting into another wave. Readjusting his rig, he rode it back toward the beach.

He splashed past Eric, who had wiped out in the wave. Eric treaded water next to his board. His mouth hung open as Nick slid by. "How did you do that?" Eric asked.

"Do what?" Nick said. He shrugged and closed in on the beach. There, people clapped and ran toward him.

Meiko was jumping up and down. "My star student!" she yelled, waving the camera above her head. When Nick hopped off the board, she gave him a hug. "That was incredible!" Meiko shrieked.

"I don't even know what happened," Nick admitted. "I thought I was going to bite it."

Meiko pushed some buttons on the camera to display the pictures she'd taken. "Look at this," she said, showing Nick one of the photos.

In the photo, Nick was flipping over.

"I did a forward loop?" Nick cried.

He couldn't believe it. But there it was, in digital color.

* * *

Back at the hotel room, Nick put the last of his clothes in the suitcase. He'd gotten Meiko's e-mail address and promised to write.

She also made him promise he'd keep windsurfing, even if it was on the lakes back home.

As Nick zipped his suitcase closed, Eric came in from the hallway.

"Hey, bro," Eric said. "Got something for you."

Eric threw a framed picture on the bed. It was the photo of Nick on his windsurfing board, flipped upside down in mid-air.

It was like an action shot from a movie. Nick couldn't help but smile.

"Thanks, Eric," Nick said.

"Yeah, well, I'm proud of you," Eric said, nodding. "You stuck with it, and look what happened. You're like a legend around here now."

Nah, Nick thought. *I'm just not a quitter. Not anymore.*

ABOUT THE AUTHOR

Thomas Kingsley Troupe is a freelance writer, filmmaker, and firefighter/EMT. He is the author of many books for kids of all ages, and he's worked on the visual effects crews of numerous feature movies. His love of action and adventure is often reflected in his stories and films. Thomas lives in Minnesota with his wife and young sons.

ABOUT THE ILLUSTRATOR

When Sean Tiffany was growing up, he lived on a small island off the coast of Maine. Every day until he graduated from high school, he had to take a boat to get to school! Sean has a pet cactus named Jim.

GLOSSARY

ADVANCED (ad-VANST)—difficult

COMPLICATED (KOM-pli-kay-tid)—difficult to do or understand

DISASTER (duh-ZASS-tur)—something that has turned out completely wrong

IMPRESSED (im-PRESST)—wowed or surprised

LEGEND (LEJ-uhnd)—an extremely famous person

NATURAL (NACH-ur-uhl)—good at something because of a special talent or ability

POLICY (POL-uh-see)—a rule

REFUNDS (RI-fuhndz)—money given back to the person who paid it

RENT (RENT)—pay money to borrow something

SUCCEED (suhk-SEED)—to do well at something

SYNCHRONIZED (SING-kruh-nized)—done at the same time

DISCUSSION QUESTIONS

1. Why didn't Nick want to learn how to surf?

2. Was it wrong for Nick to not tell his family what he was doing while he was learning to windsurf? Why or why not?

3. Do you think Nick will continue to windsurf when he gets home from Hawaii? Explain your answer.

WRITING PROMPTS

1. Pretend you're Nick. Write a letter to a friend at home, telling them about your vacation to Hawaii.

2. At the end of this book, Nick is leaving Hawaii. What do you think happens next? Write a chapter that extends the story.

3. Nick's family is vacationing in Hawaii. Where would you go if you could travel anywhere? What would you do and see there? Write about it.

WINDSURFING WORDS

BOOM (BOOM)—a piece of equipment that attaches to the mast and provides support for the sail

FOOT STRAPS (FUT STRAPS)—pieces of material that help secure a foot to a windsurfing board

FORWARD LOOP (FOR-wurd LOOP)—a flip in which the windsurfer flips forward in the air

GOGGLES (GOG-uhlz)—special glasses that fit tightly around the eyes to protect them

GUST (GUHST)—a strong, sudden blast of wind

LEASH (LEESH)—a strap or cord that connects the board to the surfer

LIFE VEST (LIFE VEST)—a special vest designed to keep the person wearing it afloat in the water if they fall in

MAST (MAST)—the tall upright post that holds the sail

RIG (RIG)—the arrangement of sails on a sailing vessel or board

YOU SHOULD KNOW

SAIL (SAYL)—a large sheet of strong cloth that makes a board, boat, or ship move when it catches the wind

STANCE (STANSS)—the way a person stands

UPHAUL (UP-hawl)—the line or rope that raises the sail

WETSUIT (WET-soot)—an item of clothing worn while surfing or swimming